THE ORCHID BOAT

Lee Harwood

THE ORCHID BOAT

To Joan Hall,
with hopes that you
will enjoy these poems
as much as I do.

Love from

Anne Stevenson

30 May, 2014

ENITHARMON PRESS

First published in 2014
by Enitharmon Press
10 Bury Place
London WC1A 2JL

www.enitharmon.co.uk

Distributed in the UK by
Central Books
99 Wallis Road
London E9 5LN

ISBN: 978-1-907587-53-5

Enitharmon Press gratefully acknowledges the financial support of
Arts Council England through Grants for the Arts.

British Library Cataloguing-in-Publication Data.
A catalogue record for this book is available
from the British Library.

Designed in Albertina by Libanus Press
and printed in England by SRP

ACKNOWLEDGEMENTS

Some of these poems have appeared in the following magazines: *English: The Journal of the English Association, London Review of Books, Poetry Wales, Shearsman* and *tall.lighthouse.*

'Naming the Names' was included in the anthology *Entailing Happiness: Friends of Robert Vas Dias celebrate his eightieth birthday* (Infinity Press, 2010). 'The Books' was first published as a booklet, with an accompanying mini-disc of its reading, by Longbarrow Press (2011). My thanks to these editors and publishers for their encouragement.

Also my thanks to Geert Mak for allowing me to quote from his book *In Europe* in the poem 'Ben's Photo'. And, of course, my thanks to Ben E. Watkins for his cover photo taken in the Piazza Maggiore, Bologna, 1992 (copyright Ben E. Watkins).

LEE HARWOOD

CONTENTS

1

DEPARTURES

A hot summer night,
the sound of rain in the courtyard.
A satin breeze   sways the curtains.

She wrote
            'Gently I open
my silk dress and float alone
on the orchid boat. Who can
take a letter beyond the clouds?' *

All those years ago

And he wrote
'A picture held us captive and we
could not get outside it.'

When the winter came
she wrote
'I put on my new quilted robe
sewn with gold thread.' **

Is that how you saw it?
Passing a mirror in a dusky corridor
– that face, the tilt of those shoulders.
Or in the bright light of morning
the details of your face in that mirror
– a picture, as though set, that maps
the wear of years, dreams,
that this is where we've come to,
and the future best left to itself.

The letter will reach the other side of the mountains,

clouds will roll back clear of the summits.
What was needed was done, but never done,
it's never done.

Plodding along the mountain path –
drifts of rain, streams sweeping across the path,
cloud so low you can barely see the path
as you stumble on loose rock.

How to imagine an orchid boat?
It gets harder. But days come and go,
the sun comes out and everything seems to sparkle
and the letter spirals away.

The picture in the mirror seemed so real,
though only caught that imprisoning moment.
A golden leaf in autumn spins into a dark river
where the currents dance it underwater back and forth, side to side.

Without thinking
I step aboard the orchid boat,
the feel of silk
carrying me beyond all mirrors.

* from the poem 'Sorrows of Departure' by the Chinese poet Li Ch'ing-Chao
(c. 1084 – c. 1151).
** from the poem 'A Song of Departure' by Li Ch'ing-Chao.

A cold wind sweeps down from the mountains and along this wide empty valley. In the distance a traction engine, pulling two wagons, crosses a dry riverbed strewn with boulders and bleached branches. The wool jackets of the two men are black with dirt and grease. Their faces blurred, but clear as you approach. When close up the maker's name on the engine's side is just discernible below the grime.

The bulging canvas over the wagons covers ... Who knows what? Soft goods for the 'outback'? Maybe bales of wool to buy comfort and small pleasures? Everyone a small trader at heart.

And after that moment? that journey? After success or failure or just the usual steady working through the days? A century later

Lying in bed thinking about when I'll die, how I'll die. In the middle of the night or some early afternoon when walking in a town or by the sea or in the usual hospital mess?

'I don't want to be here'

stumbling around in and out of history.

No answers to that one.

'You should get out more.'

A fine rain closes in as I hunker down in the shelter of a rock fall.

And in North East India the Khasi people still sing some hymns in Welsh.

ORNITHOLOGY

A wall of dense fog ahead
– blocked, all knowledge denied.
'The flying bird brings the message.'
What message from out there?
('Chirpy chirpy cheep cheep' doesn't help much.)

Flying low it sweeps over the meadows
hunting small insects then moves on
heading north to settle
for a while.

The worn book advises small steps
and a slow care. Nothing too fancy.
Some form of change ahead, it says.

A silence on the hillside. All this whiteness.
A stillness in which time has ceased, or seems so.

As the mist shifts you see swallows set on a wire,
a wagtail bobbing on a rock.

THE BOOKS

'She climbed down from the tree the next day   a queen'
after many adventures.
Beyond the wood a field sloped down to a wide river,
its banks edged with reeds.

And at the frontier?
that mixture of squalor and bureaucratic inefficiency.
Is this Europe or China or a dusty crossing in Mexico?
It could be. In a story or at this moment?

She climbed down from the tree a queen,
her memories pleasant for now, but later?
As the years slide by (passing a mirror
– who is that old woman? ugly old man?)
other memories heap up, crowd in.
The intense pain of partings, foolishness, selfishness,
stubborn blindness, and useless, though real, regrets.
As though caught below decks in a sinking ship,
water pouring in as further leaks spring,
the metal plates buckle and split.
Memory pouring in. Powerless to stop any of it.

You can go into the books.
Remember the library in Alexandria.
Remember its destruction by Christian fanatics,
and the savage murder of the mathematician Hypatia.
(Bishop Cyril, may you be tormented forever
in your imaginary hell. You and that other dark heart
Archbishop Theophilus.   Shame on you all.)

A dense history of such deeds,
but that shrinks into the shadows
when faced with our daily history.

The young officer, my father, 1940,
having to shoot one of his own men,
his stomach ripped open beyond saving,
begging to be put out of his agony.

'We deceive ourselves with our stories', someone wrote.
Not this one. How did my father
live with that moment for years and years?
as he quietly tended his allotment, and
taught children mathematics.

She climbed down from the tree a queen.
As we all do, and then set out
across golden stubble to the river.

I don't intend to sit here waiting in my coffin,
gathering dust until the final slammer,
adjusting my tiara.

I'll stamp my foot
and, checking the rear-view mirror,
head for the frontier.

2

OBJECTS ON A POLISH TABLE

1

Four books, two newspapers,
an ashtray, a pack of cigarettes, matches.

2

when visitors are coming
some poppy seed cake or doughnuts
or fresh baked makaroniki
placed on a plate on the table

a lace table cloth beneath the coffee cups

3

a ceramic salt bowl with a lid

4

an empty vase in the centre of
the oil cloth

Come and sit down

LEAH LAFORGUE

I'll tell you a story. There was a draper in Teignmouth, Devon, named Samuel Lee (1826-95). He and his wife Leah (née Page, 1832–83) had 18 children. One of his sons was Herbert Lee (1859–1924), my great grandfather. One of Samuel Lee's daughters was Leah Lee (1861-88). Leah, as a young woman, went to Berlin where she lived teaching English. One of her students was the poet Jules Laforgue (1860–87) who was then French Reader to the Empress Augusta. In 1886 they married, left Berlin and moved to Paris for Laforgue to pursue his literary career. She must have been a 'romantic soul' and 'spirited' as they say. In Paris Laforgue grew increasingly ill with tuberculosis and died on the 20th of August 1887. Leah Lee, who had nursed him throughout his illness, also caught tuberculosis and died the following year on the 6th of June.

I'm not making this up.

WINCHESTER POND

for Lindy

Through green water
the old frog swims up from the muddy bottom
to the glitter of sunlight on the pond's surface.

His orange eyes bright with expectation. It's a good day.
The story of the lotus may be of interest,
but time for fun and pleasure.

A few strokes, a fly or two,
a wander through the long grass on the bank.

Anthropomorphism isn't much use, is it?
Wishful thinking.
I haven't got green skin.

Meanwhile those innocent moments
as I curl round you in the night.

CHILDISH

From the top balcony of a pagoda
in the Royal Botanic Gardens
you step
                                out into the air,
step from treetop to treetop
then swoop through the air to further trees
– as a bird, though not – and
on bright spring days shoot up to
those glittering white clouds and
walk the skies.

These day dreams that carry you through.

And to the south,
late one evening on a balcony by the sea,
a note flutters down   written by a child.
It says 'Do not disturb the angel'.

Words like that shower of sparks
as welders hunch over their job
cutting and joining beams.

So much hope in such moments
wherever they may happen
without reason or purpose, but there.

The gardens spread off into a green haze of trees,
woods that may border a river or a busy city road.
A calm as you gaze into an unknown distance.

Late at night standing, watching.
The sound of the waves breaking on the shore,
the lights of passing freighters out to sea.

The next morning the red handrail of the pagoda
glistens with raindrops.

A STEADY LIGHT

Mid-afternoon   a light breeze
sways the worn blue curtain.

Could this be Alexandria?
– I think not –
but some provincial city? seaport?
And the year?

In a cluttered office, dust on the ledges,
the books in perfect order, the accounts all up to date,
the correspondence answered and filed.

Evening dreams   stories of emperors and patriarchs,
stories of moments when it could have been different
but wasn't. Constantine XI Palaeologus,
the last emperor, falling in battle
at the fall of Constantinople, the end of Byzantium,
overwhelmed by the relentless force of Sultan Mehmet II.

Overwhelmed by years of broken promises and betrayals,
of petty ambitions and selfish blindness,
under those eggshell domes and rounded arches.
The glint of gold mosaics in dark corners.
A line of ikons where saints stare into another world.
Elaborate robes and rituals and attempts at clarity,
listing the laws in many volumes, the science and philosophy,
all copied, copied again, amended, copied again,
to keep the barbarians at bay whether Frankish or Turk or . . .
One thousand, one hundred and twenty-three years of this.

A curtain stirs in the tired room
while the same breeze slowly shifts
the hangings in the nearby hospital.
Distant sounds from the streets below.

Get up from the couch or chair.
Walk across the room to stop by the window.
The air heavy with the heat of summer.

How true is your heart?
We all know the jackal waits for a spare feather.
And a choir sings

        'People get ready for
        the train to Jordan.'

3

PALAEONTOLOGY

On the edge of town the half finished buildings,
a red neon sign flickering in the distance.
You step off into the scrub, an abandoned orchard.
The thick summer darkness, crickets whirring.

Was this where you expected to end up?
lost or mainly so?   in a dream?
Planks scattered on the ground,
cement smeared shuttering just left.

But the night not *that* frightening,
the landscape well known despite the strangeness.
Been-here-before one way or another.
To push on past weariness, but with so much baggage.

You know?   and . . .
You cry out in your sleep.
Why, how is that?
'Carelessness is also disastrous', someone wrote.

An ice-coated ledge or a small neglect
decades ago when a little clarity . . .
A daily haunting, a nightly haunting.
Heavy with memories.

Ordering the ordinary – that surface stuff –
move the chair, safely put away that dish
– but below, gnawing at the foundations,
ignorance or just avoiding the questions.

To stand back from bare times – alive and alert –
'Shall we exchange gifts now?'
looking up at the night sky – that simplicity.
A street light seen through the branches.

Here comes Mrs Trilobite, fresh from the shale.
She'll shake the nonsense out of us.

NAMING THE NAMES

Sailing across the bay to the outer islands,
a bright blustery day (I imagine this), and
all the pain of history just blows away.

Shall we have white sails? or blue? or Brixham red?
And back in the harbour the masts crowd together.
'Blue Shadow', 'Red Duster', 'Imfrey', 'Lumpy Custard'.

At night a drift of clouds, but the stars so bright –
Orion's Belt, The Plough, maybe The Little Dipper.
The flash of a distant lighthouse. Beyond this . . . it wavers.
                                                    And in the city?

Back and forth across the oceans to those continents
cluttered with so much stuff, whether it be simply
shoes and plates, books and pictures, or not so simply.

As the years pass so lost at times in those familiar streets.
A weight of memories, or just another
casual bombing and strafing raid across the Channel.

Did you know what was happening then? A child
who's taken to see where the V1 rocket landed,
where a row of six houses had disappeared.

At such a distance there's no knowing except
the sound of crunching glass as you're carried
across the bedroom, window blown in across the bed,

that's always remembered. In a quiet room somewhere,
sunlight and . . .   On the spread-out map
all the gradations of blue.

Amazed at the colours

for Robert Vas Dias on his 80th birthday

BEN'S PHOTO

for Kelvin Corcoran

Just off the main square
at the entrance to a crowded narrow street
– this is in Bologna, 1992 –
a man stood erect, hands behind his back,
watching something, or just waiting.

A man about 60 or 70, wearing a cloth cap,
an old suit jacket, a worn but neatly ironed shirt,
neatly buttoned. No tie.
An afternoon in winter.

Don't know why. This moment that keeps
coming back. Not haunting, but something else.

One pauses. As he did.

Through the mirror that other world,
almost like this? The colours maybe softer?
the world there harsher? The strangeness,

both sides, of a face, a scene.
What's there before and beyond the glass,
but somehow outside. Beyond the fear.

One pauses.
'Wait for the right time', but when is that?
And what **does** the book mean?

You pick up a cup, taste the coffee,
put down the cup. That moment midway
between cup and lips. A timeless pause.

With Japanese calligraphy you hold the brush,
elbow tight to your body, move your whole body
to make the marks. A flow of sorts.

Paint the character for 'sea' again and again.
What's the character for 'man under arch'?
Stood there swaying, brush in hand.

'That was a close one.'   Stood swaying,
after the event, then shifting to a calm
where a cup or a curtain stirred by the wind
or a patch of winter sunlight spread in the street
becomes a marvel.

You were so close to the exit.
Yes, people carry on. In that narrow street
a crowd watching a TV in a shop window.

'A British officer, William Pressey, reported seeing
200 French cavalrymen advancing across a hilltop
close to Amiens, a stirring sight with their plumed
helmets and gleaming lances. "They laughed and waved
their lances to us, shouting "Le Bosch fini", "Death
to the Kraut". Just after they disappeared from sight
he heard the dry rattle of machine guns. Only a few
stray horses came back.'*

Put the cup down on the saucer.

Looking up – remote but close –
you see the afternoon sun catch
a row of jars and bottles on a shelf.

Thankful for this moment.

* from Geert Mak, *In Europe*.

IT ALL COMES BACK TO VASSILIS TSITSANIS

It's near quiet in the empty room at night.
Maybe the sound of distant cars
or rain beating on the window.

'Welcome to the orphanage.'

In the forest a darkness that's
edged by moonlight now
the showers have passed, leaving
a damp chill on the faint track
that reaches a gate and open country.

'Where are the orphans' toys kept?'

In silence the shooting stars fly over
the nearby mountains.

A building in the distance, with
rain beating on its windows? As mystified
as I. And then when morning comes
the walk down to the shore. Banks
of grey clouds low over a grey sea.

To think back to a cloudy Sunday,
the necessary code in the words sung.
'You make my heart bleed
. . . I can't find a moment's peace.' *
Photos of burnt villages and the few
inhabitants when the lorries have gone.
'fear overshadowed everything' he said.

While a long way away the toys and books
piled in a cupboard, undisturbed for now.

'Now, say "thank you" nicely.'

Alone in the noisy corridors
the child, as though sleepwalking,
other children running by, moves towards
the cupboard and then his room.
Clouds bringing rain. A distant
distorted music.

*from Tsitanis's song 'Cloudy Sunday', written in Athens 1943–44.

THE OAK COFFER

for my uncle, Alfred Miles 1909–1987

'they created a desert, and they call it peace' *
and that could have been said of Carthage,
though it wasn't. It was much closer to home.
Scattered blocks of stone, and dust, the stumps of houses.
And now left with men who lie, no matter what,
for little reason, vanity or fear,
but who lie, amid smiling cruelty.

'Now how will the little people get out of this one?'

There was a stagnation, the lily pond clogged with weed,
fish deformed, as people drift, as I drift.
Some forms of inertia and indifference

while every Saturday morning you polished
the oak coffer, week after week.
The scent of beeswax in that narrow hall.
The wood polished till you could see your face in it.
A decent man who'd always been told what to do.

It goes so deep, the anger and unspoken stories.
To curse 'the bosses'?   That's another story,
and along with all its contradictions.

Your father – ex-soldier and drunk,
at times a gardener at Windsor Castle –
who in hard times put his children in an orphanage.
But you survived in one way, though with
so much missing.   'We manage.'

To gently run your finger along the edge
of the wood as you pass by.
Keep this memory close of dear virtue.

'Say that to me quietly.'

You made a toy fort from scraps of wood,
painted it late on winter evenings
when the child was asleep.
The steady drone of bombers overhead.
The years pass. Beyond the plywood walls,
out in the open, grief woven in our hearts.
Martha Mavroidi sing, we may get through.

* from a speech by Galgacus, one of the Caledonian leaders, protesting
at the Roman invasion of North Britain, as reported by Tacitus in
Agricola, book 1 (30).

SAILING WESTWARDS

Centuries ago the sages plod up the ivory mountain,
up rock–cut steps, past battered pines,
to the summit shrine to pay their respects,
mist in the valley below, a soft breeze.

Later, I – no sage – reach a summit cairn,
add a stone here for you, Paul,
as ravens glide by, two buzzards circle,
and a flock of goats clatters across the scree below.

Whether the T'ien-t'ai Mountains
or the rough world of the Rhinog,
what the Italian poet called 'the immensity'?
or at least a peace – the sun slowly setting –

far away from that bitter taste.
Smoke drifting from a giant incense burner
carried by four grimacing demons,
pride and anger in their hearts. (Bronze, 19th century.)

The dowager empress sharpening her nails
while in the kitchens the workers scurry around,
maybe laughing quietly, and in remote fields
villagers hoe and plant, haul heavy loads.

On a street corner, as crowds flow by,
'What are you doing?'   'Nothing in particular.'
A few more years to go. But then suddenly
that music plays, lifts me to I know not where.

So where's the boat?
A sampan or a lugger?
or an elegant steam launch?
Is there room for me and that crew of sages?

Zig-zag around, as usual.
What's to be seen in the old woman's curio cabinet?
Ivory carvings, plates, cups, and a blue glass sugar-shaker.
We just don't know the full story.

On the vast beach at Harlech
scattered with tellin shells and razor-shells,
dunes topped with marram grass behind me
and the dark blue grey mountains behind them,

and the flat silk sea spreads out in front of me,
over and far beyond the horizon.

4

Star of our hearts aS, dear precious child,

the moons slowly glide Through clouds while

the trees tremblE against a night sky.

Lying now in your crib cLear-eyed, your clear beauty

leads us back to marveL, to a near wordless joy

as we think of what dreAms will pass through your head.

for Stella Isabel Harwood-Marshall
born 21st July 2010